Pour Alice, princesse Li Tsou,

et Louitou, type formidab'

the eye of the wolf

the eye of the wolf

Daniel Pennac

translated by Sarah Ardizzone

illustrated by Max Grafe

foreword by Michael Morpurgo

WALKER
BOOKS

First published 2002 by Walker Books Ltd
87 Vauxhall Walk, London SE11 5HJ

This edition published 2014

4 6 8 10 9 7 5 3

Original edition: *L'Oeil du Loup*

This book is supported by the French Ministry for Foreign Affairs, as part of the Burgess programme headed for the French Embassy in London by the Institut Français du Royaume-Uni

This book has been typeset in Weiss and Aquinas

Printed and bound in Great Britain by Clays Ltd, St Ives plc

British Library Cataloguing in Publication Data:
a catalogue record for this book
is available from the British Library

ISBN 978-1-4063-5257-3

www.walker.co.uk

Foreword

Most certainly Daniel Pennac's story is richly and deeply imagined. He cannot write any other way. But this is not simply a wonderful story, told with his accustomed insight and ingenuity. All this we might expect from Pennac.

In *The Eye of the Wolf* he does a rare and wonderful thing, he invites us into the mind's eye of one of the greatest storymakers of our age. Through Pennac's eye we see into the mind's eye of a wolf, go with him on his journey from the wild to the zoo. Pennac is the boy looking up into the eye of the wolf in his cage, reading the memories. And then, deftly, elegantly, Pennac is the wolf looking back down into the eye of the boy, reading his mind and his soul, following him on his journey from Africa to the zoo. And we witness through Pennac the miracle of the survival of these two, and understand their instinctive empathy as we discover how their lives have been entwined.

Pennac never tells too much. He gives respect to his readers, allows us to use our mind's eye as we read. This is storymaking at its very best, telling, subtle, moving. Simply wonderful.

Michael Morpurgo
March 2014

How They Met

I

The boy standing in front of the wolf's cage doesn't move a muscle. The wolf paces backwards and forwards. He walks the length of the enclosure and back again without stopping.

He's starting to get on my nerves, the wolf thinks to himself. For the last two hours the boy has been standing in front of the wire fencing, as still as a frozen tree, watching the wolf walking.

What does he want from me? the wolf wonders. The boy makes him feel curious. He's not worried (because wolves aren't afraid of anything), just curious. What does he want?

The other children jump and run about, shout and burst into tears, stick their tongues out at the wolf and hide their heads in their mums' skirts. Then they make silly faces in front of the gorilla's cage, or roar at the lion as he whips the air with his tail. But this boy is different. He stands there silently, without moving a muscle. Only his eyes shift. They follow the wolf as he paces the length of his wire fencing.

What's your problem? Haven't you ever seen a wolf before?

The wolf only sees the boy every other time he passes him. That's because the wolf only has one eye. He lost the other one ten years ago in a fight against humans, the day he was captured. So on his outward journey (if you can call it a journey) the wolf sees the zoo with all its cages, the children making faces and, standing in the middle of it all, the boy who doesn't move a muscle. On the return journey (if you can call it a journey) the wolf sees the inside of his enclosure. It's an empty enclosure, because the she-wolf died last week. It's a sad enclosure with a solitary rock and a dead tree. When the wolf turns round, there's the boy again, breathing steadily, his white breath hanging in the cold air.

He'll give up before I do, thinks the wolf, and he carries on walking. I'm more patient than he is, he adds. I'm the wolf.

II

But the first thing the wolf sees when he wakes up the next day is the boy, standing in exactly the same spot in front of his enclosure. The wolf nearly jumps out of his fur.

He can't have spent the night here!

He calms down and begins to pace again, as if it is nothing out of the ordinary.

The wolf's been walking for an hour now. And the boy's eyes have been following him for an hour. The wolf's blue fur brushes against the wire fencing. His muscles ripple beneath his winter coat. The blue wolf keeps on walking as if nothing will ever stop him. As if he's on his way back home to Alaska, where he comes from. The metal plaque fixed to his cage reads ALASKAN WOLF. And there's a map of the Far North, with an area marked in red: ALASKAN WOLF, BARREN LANDS.

His paws don't make a sound when they touch the ground. He moves from one end of the enclosure to the other, like a silent pendulum inside a grandfather clock. The boy's eyes move slowly, as if he's following a game of tennis in slow motion.

Does he really think I'm *that* interesting?

The wolf frowns. The bristles on his muzzle stand on end. He's annoyed with himself for asking so many questions. He swore not to have anything more to do with human beings. He's been true to his word for ten years now: he hasn't thought about human beings once, or even glanced at them. He has cut himself off completely. He doesn't look at the kids making silly faces in front of his cage, or the zookeeper throwing him his meat from a distance, or the artists drawing him on Sundays, or the stupid mums showing him to their toddlers and squawking, "Look at the big bad wolf! He'll gobble you up if you're naughty!" He doesn't look at any of them.

"Not even the best human beings are worth bothering about." That's what Black Flame, the wolf's mother, always used to say.

Sometimes the wolf would take a break from

pacing. Up until last week, that is. He and the she-wolf would sit facing the visitors. It was as if they couldn't see them. He and the she-wolf would stare straight ahead. They stared straight through them. It made the visitors feel like they didn't even exist. It was spooky.

"What are they looking at in that strange way?"

"What can they see?"

But then the she-wolf, who was grey and white like a snow partridge, died. The wolf hasn't stopped moving since. He walks from morning to evening, and leaves his meat to freeze on the ground. Outside, straight as the letter i (imagine the dot is his white breath hanging in the air), the boy watches him.

If that's the way he wants it, that's his problem, the wolf decides. And he stops thinking about the boy altogether.

III

But the next day the boy is there again. And the following day. And the day after that. Until the wolf can't help thinking about him again. Who is he? What does he want from me? Doesn't he have anything to do all day? Doesn't he have work to do? Or school to go to? Hasn't he got any friends? Or parents? Or relatives?

So many questions slow his pace; his legs feel heavy. He's not worn out yet, but he might be soon. Unbelievable! thinks the wolf.

At least the zoo will be closed tomorrow. Once a month there's a special day when the zookeepers check on the animals' health and repair their cages. No visitors are allowed.

That'll get him off my back.

Wrong again. The next day, just like all the other days, the boy is there. He seems to be more present than ever – all alone in front of the enclosure, all alone in an empty zoo.

Oh, no, groans the wolf. But that's the way it is.

The wolf is starting to feel worn out now. The boy's stare seems to weigh a ton. All right, thinks the wolf. You've asked for it! And suddenly he stops walking. He sits bolt upright opposite the boy. And he starts staring back. He doesn't look through him. It's a real stare, a *fixed* stare.

So now they're opposite each other.

And they just keep on staring.

There isn't a single visitor in the zoo. The vets haven't arrived yet. The lions haven't come out of their lair. The birds are asleep under their feathers. It's a day of rest for everyone. Even the monkeys have stopped making mischief. They hang from the branches like sleeping bats.

There's just the boy.

And the wolf with the blue fur.

So you want to stare at me? Fine! I'll stare at you too. And we'll soon see...

But there's something bothering the wolf. A silly detail. He's only got one eye and the boy's got two. The wolf doesn't know which of the boy's eyes to stare into. He hesitates. His single eye jumps: right-left, left-right. The boy's eyes don't flinch. He doesn't flutter an eyelash. The wolf feels extremely uneasy. He won't turn his head away for the whole world. And there's no question of starting to pace again. His eye begins to lose control. Soon, across the scar of his dead eye, a tear appears. Not because he's sad, but out of a sense of helplessness and anger.

So the boy does something strange that calms the wolf and makes him feel more at ease. The boy closes an eye.

Now they're looking into each other's eye, in a zoo that's silent and empty, and they've got all the time in the world.

The Eye of the Wolf

I

The wolf's yellow eye is large and round, with a black pupil in the middle. And it never blinks. The boy could be watching a candle flame in the dark. All he can see is the eye: the trees, the zoo and the enclosure have disappeared. All that's left is the eye of the wolf. It grows fatter and rounder, like a harvest moon in an empty sky. The pupil in the middle grows darker, and he can make out small coloured flecks in the yellow-brown iris – a speck of blue here, like frozen water below the sky; a glimmer of gold there, shiny as straw.

But what really matters is the pupil. The black pupil. You wanted to stare at me, it seems to be saying, so go ahead, stare at me! It sparkles so brightly, it's scary. Like a flame.

That's what it is, thinks the boy, a *black flame*! Then he answers, "All right, Black Flame, I'm staring at you and I'm not frightened."

The pupil blazes like fire as it fills the eye. But no matter how fat it gets, the boy never looks away. When everything has become pitch black, he discovers what nobody has ever seen in the wolf's eye before: *the pupil is alive.* There, staring and growling at the boy, is a black she-wolf snuggled up with her cubs. She doesn't move, but you can tell she's tense as a thunderstorm under her shiny fur. Her gums are pulled back to expose her dazzling fangs; her paws are twitching. She's ready to pounce. She'd swallow a small boy like him in a single mouthful.

"So you're really not frightened?"

That's right. The boy stays where he is. He doesn't look away. Slowly Black Flame allows her muscles to relax. After a while she whispers between her fangs, "Fine, we'll make a deal. You can stare as much as you like, if that's the way you want it, but don't disturb me while I'm teaching the little ones – is that clear?" And, without sparing the boy another thought, she casts a careful eye over the seven fluffy cubs asleep around her. They form a red-tinged halo.

The iris, thinks the boy, the iris around the pupil...

Five of the cubs are exactly the same rust-red colour as the iris. The sixth one has blue-red fur, as blue as frozen water under a clear sky. He's called Blue Wolf. And the seventh, a little yellow she-wolf, is like a ray of gold. It makes your eyes crinkle just to look at her. Her brothers call her Shiny Straw.

All around them lies the snow. It stretches as far as the hills on the horizon. The silent snow of Alaska in the Far North.

Black Flame's voice rises solemnly out of the white silence. "Children, today I'm going to talk to you about human beings."

II

"Humans?"

"Again?"

"Boring!"

"You're always telling us stories about humans."

"We've heard enough!"

"We're not babies!"

"Why don't you tell us about caribou, or snow rabbits, or duck-hunting?"

"Yes, Black Flame, tell us a hunting story."

"Wolves are hunters, so give us a hunting story."

But Shiny Straw's cries can be heard above all the rest. "No, I want a real story about humans, a scary story. Please, Mum, please, I love human stories!"

Only Blue Wolf keeps quiet. He's not much of a talker. In fact, he's rather serious. A bit sad you might say. Even his brothers think he's too serious. But on the rare occasions when he speaks, everyone listens. He's as wise as an old wolf with battle scars.

Picture the scene: the five Redheads are scrapping – going for each other's throats, jumping on each other's backs, snapping at each other's legs, chasing their own tails in crazy circles … it's mayhem. Shiny Straw cheers them on in her high-pitched voice, jumping up and down on the spot like a frog in spring. And silver glints of snow fly all around them.

Black Flame just lets them get on with it. They might as well enjoy themselves while they can; they'll find out how tough a wolf's life is soon enough. She glances at Blue Wolf, the only one of her children who never fools around. The spitting image of his father. This thought makes her feel proud and sad at the same time because Great Wolf, his father, is dead.

Too serious, thinks Black Flame. Too much of a worrier… Too much of a wolf…

"Listen!" Blue Wolf is sitting as still as a rock, his front legs stiff and his ears pricked up. "Listen!"

The scrapping stops straight away. The snow begins to settle again around the cubs. They can't hear anything to begin with. The Redheads strain their furry ears, but all they can make out is the sudden moaning of the wind, like a frozen tongue licking them.

And then, all of a sudden, the long, modulated howl of a wolf is heard behind the wind, and it speaks volumes.

"It's Grey Cousin," whispers one of the Redheads.

"What's he saying?"

Black Flame glances quickly at Blue Wolf. Both of them know what Grey Cousin is telling them from the hilltop where he's standing guard.

Men! A band of hunters... Trying to track them down. The same band as last time.

"The game's over now, children. Get ready – we're leaving!"

III

So was that how you spent your childhood, Blue Wolf: trying to escape from bands of hunters?

Yes, it was. We settled in a peaceful valley surrounded by hills that Grey Cousin thought no human could climb over. We stayed there for a week or two, but then we had to move on again. The men refused to give up. The same band had been on our family's trail for two moons. They'd already got Great Wolf, our father – not without a struggle, but they got him in the end.

So we made a hasty escape. We walked in single file. Black Flame led the procession, followed by me, Blue Wolf. Then came Shiny Straw and the Redheads. And, bringing up the rear, Grey Cousin wiped away the footprints with his tail. We never left any marks. We vanished completely as we pushed on deeper into the north. It grew colder. The snow turned to ice; the rocks became sharp as knives. But the men still managed to track us down.

They were always on our heels. No obstacle was too great for them. Those men… Human beings…

At night they slept in foxes' dens. (Foxes are always willing to lend their dens to wolves. They do it for food, because they're too lazy to hunt for themselves.) Grey Cousin would keep watch outside, sitting on a rock overlooking the valley. Blue Wolf would sleep at the entrance to the den. Right at the back, Black Flame would tell the little cubs stories until they fell asleep. They were human stories, of course. Because it was night-time and they were too tired to play any more, because they loved being scared and Black Flame was there to protect them, Shiny Straw and the Redheads listened.

Once upon a time…

It was always the same story about a clumsy cub and his aged grandmother:

Once upon a time there lived a cub who was *so* clumsy he'd never caught anything in his life.

Even the oldest caribou ran too quickly for him, field mice got away from right under his nose, and ducks flew within a whisker of his muzzle. He couldn't even catch his own tail! He was just *too* clumsy.

But he had to be good at something, didn't he? Fortunately he had a granny who was very old. She was *so* old she couldn't catch anything either. Her big sad eyes would watch the young wolves running. Her skin no longer quivered at the scent of game. Everybody felt sorry for her.

They left her behind in the lair when they went off hunting. Slowly she would do the tidying up, before washing herself with great care. She had a magnificent coat. It was silver, and it was all that remained of her youth. No other wolf had ever had such a beautiful coat. When she'd finished washing herself – it took her at least two hours – Granny would lie down at the entrance to the lair, with her muzzle between her paws, waiting for Clumsy to come back. It was Clumsy's job to feed Granny. The haunch of the first caribou killed always went to Granny.

"Are you sure it's not too heavy for you, Clumsy?"

"Of course not!"

"Make sure you don't dawdle on the way back."

"And don't trip over your paws!"

"And steer clear of humans."

And so on.

Clumsy had given up listening to all this advice. He knew what he was doing.

Until one day when—

"Until one day when what?" asked the Redheads, their big eyes dilated in the dark.

"When what? When what?" squeaked Shiny Straw with her tongue hanging out.

Black Flame's voice came in a terrifying whisper:

Until one day when a man reached the lair before Clumsy did.

"And then what?"

"And then what? Go on... What happened next?"

The man killed Granny, stole her fur to make a coat, stole her ears to make a hat and turned her muzzle into a mask.

"And what happened after that?"

"You'll find out when I tell you the rest tomorrow. It's time for bed now, children."

The cubs complained, but Black Flame was firm. Gradually drowsy sounds filled the lair. Blue Wolf always waited for this moment to ask his question. And he always asked the same thing.

"Was that a true story, Black Flame?"

Black Flame would pause and consider before giving the same strange reply. "Let's just say, more true than not."

IV

The seasons came and went, and the cubs grew into young wolves and skilful hunters. But they'd never seen a human being. Not close up, at any rate. They'd heard the noises humans make. On the day Great Wolf fought his battle against them, for example. They'd heard Great Wolf howling, and a man roaring with pain at fangs sunk into his backside. They'd heard the shouts of panic, the orders barked out, something that sounded like a clap of thunder and then ... nothing. Great Wolf never came back.

So they found themselves on the run again.

They'd seen them from a distance. No sooner had they left a valley than the humans settled in. The valley would begin to smoke like a cauldron.

"They're dirtying the snow," complained Black Flame.

They watched them from the top of the highest

hill. They could see them walking on two feet at the bottom of the cauldron. But what did they look like close up?

"Grey Cousin, you've seen them close up before, haven't you?"

"I've seen some of them, yes." Grey Cousin didn't talk much.

"What do they look like?"

"Humans? Two legs and a gun."

That was all they could get out of him.

And Black Flame told them stories they no longer believed in now they were grown up. "Humans eat everything: the grass that caribou eat, as well as the caribou themselves. They'll even eat wolves if they haven't got anything else to fill their bellies!" Or, "Human beings have two skins: the first is naked without a single patch of fur, and the second is like ours." Or, "What is a human being? A human being is a collector." (Nobody understood what she meant by this.)

One day, while they paused for a moment to catch their breath, someone asked, "Why is it always the *same* band that's after us?"

Grey Cousin licked his bruised paws. "They've

heard about a little she-wolf with golden fur—"

Black Flame cut him off in mid-sentence with a withering look. But it was too late. All the Redheads were looking at Shiny Straw. And Shiny Straw was looking at everybody else, her ears pricked up.

"What do you mean? They're looking for *me*?"

The sun chose precisely that moment to burst through the clouds. A ray fell on Shiny Straw and everyone glanced away. She looked stunning: a golden she-wolf with a black smudge on the tip of her muzzle. Her nose was so black against the gold, she seemed to squint a bit.

She's simply gorgeous, thought Black Flame. My daughter is gorgeous. And then she added, But a complete dreamer. She sighed and a voice deep down inside her whispered, Honestly, Great Wolf, why did you have to give me the most beautiful she-wolf the world has ever seen? Don't you think we've got enough to worry about?

V

"What do you mean? They're looking for *me?"*

The strange voice in which Shiny Straw asked her question hadn't escaped Blue Wolf's ears.

"They're looking for *me?"*

Don't be so silly, of course they're not... But it was worrying, all the same...

Blue Wolf didn't know what to make of his sister. She was a beautiful she-wolf, of course. So beautiful she took your breath away. And as a hunter she was in a league of her own. She was much quicker than the Redheads, who were no mean hunters themselves. She had a better eye than Black Flame. A better ear than Grey Cousin. And, Blue Wolf was forced to admit, a more sensitive muzzle than me. She would come to an abrupt halt with her nose in the air and say, "There's a prairie mouse!"

"Where?"

"Over there!" She would point to a specific

spot three hundred metres away. When they reached it, they would find a family of red-backed prairie mice as plump as partridges tucked underground.

The Redheads could never get over it. "How did you guess?"

"My nose," she would reply.

Or in the summer, when they were hunting ducks... The Redheads would swim soundlessly towards their prey, with only the tips of their noses sticking out. They never made a ripple. But nine times out of ten the ducks would fly away from right under their noses. Shiny Straw would stay on the river bank, flat as a cat in the yellow grass. And she would wait. The ducks would take off heavily, skimming the water. When the fattest duck flew over her head – action! One leap, one snap of her teeth.

"How did you manage that?"

"My eyes!"

And when it was time for the caribou to migrate and the herd was spread right across the plain... The wolves would climb to the top of the highest hill, and Shiny Straw would say, "The sixth on the right from the big rock is sick." (Wolves have a rule

that they only eat sick caribou.)

"He's sick? How can you be sure?"

"My ears! Listen," she would add. "He's having difficulty breathing."

She could even catch polar hares – something no other wolf had ever managed before.

"My legs!"

But despite these feats Shiny Straw missed the simplest opportunities. For instance, she'd be chasing an old caribou that was huffing and puffing, when all of a sudden she'd switch her attention to a snow partridge flying overhead. Looking up, she'd trip over her own feet. Then her face would crumple and they'd find her rolling around on the ground, shrieking with laughter like a baby cub.

"You laugh too much," Blue Wolf would complain. "You don't take anything seriously."

"And you're too serious; you never see the funny side of things."

Blue Wolf didn't like this kind of answer. "Why do you laugh so much, Shiny Straw?"

She would stop laughing, look Blue Wolf straight in the eye and reply, "Because I'm bored."

And she would explain. "Nothing ever happens in this stupid country; nothing ever changes!"

And then she would repeat, "I'm bored."

VI

And it was because she was bored that Shiny Straw wanted to see something new. She wanted to see what human beings looked like close up. One night she finally got her chance. The same band of hunters was still hot on the family's trail. They had pitched camp in a grassy basin three hours away from the lair. Shiny Straw could smell the smoke from their fires. She could even hear the dry wood crackling.

That's it, I'm off, she said to herself. I'll be back before dawn. I'll get to see what they look like at last. I'll have a story to tell to make life more interesting for everyone. I'm the one they're looking for, after all…

She seemed to have plenty of good reasons. And off she went.

She had already been gone an hour when Blue

Wolf woke up in the night, sensing that something was wrong. He guessed straight away. She was crafty enough to dupe Grey Cousin, who was on watch, and she would have headed off towards the men.

I've got to catch up with her, he thought.

But Blue Wolf didn't manage to catch up with her.

When he reached the hunters' camp, he saw the men dancing in the firelight around a net tied with a thick rope to a sort of wooden gallows. Shiny Straw was caught in the net and was furiously gnashing her teeth. Flashes of gold glanced off her fur in the darkness. Dogs jumped up and down in a frenzy of excitement below the net. They were yapping and yelping. The men let out great cries as they danced. They were clad in wolfskins.

Black Flame was right, thought Blue Wolf. He paused. If I bite the rope, the net will land in the middle of those dogs. She's too fast for them, and we'll make our getaway.

He had to jump over the fires, which is something wolves don't like doing. But it was the only way, and it had to be done quickly. There was no time to be scared. He had to catch them by surprise.

He was already high in the burning air, above the flames, above the men (whose faces looked very red in the firelight) and above the net. He ripped the rope with one tug of his teeth and shouted, "Run, Shiny Straw!"

The men and their dogs were still looking up in the night air, confused.

Shiny Straw hesitated. "I'm sorry, Blue Wolf, I—"

And then it was pandemonium. Blue Wolf drove two dogs into the flames. "Run, and look after the family!"

Blue Wolf saw Shiny Straw take an enormous leap. Then he heard those thunderclaps. The snow around her was splattered with little craters. Missed! She disappeared into the night.

Blue Wolf didn't have a second to celebrate. A bear-sized man was standing in front of him waving a flaming branch. The blow came as a shock. Blue Wolf felt his head was exploding. Then there was darkness. It was a darkness filled with stars, and he was falling, falling, falling and spinning round.

VII

When he woke up he could only open one eye. They hadn't killed him. His fur had been too badly damaged in the struggle to be sold, so he ended up in the zoo. Or rather, in several zoos. Over the next ten years he stayed in five or six. Sometimes the ground was concrete and the roof was made of corrugated iron. Sometimes the ground was bare earth and there was clear sky above. He'd been in small cages and behind thick bars, in large enclosures and penned in by wire meshing. His meat was thrown to him from a distance. People came to paint him on Sundays; children were scared of him. The seasons came and went...

He was all alone. Surrounded by animals he didn't know, who were also caged off.

"A human being is a collector."

Now he understood the meaning of Black Flame's words.

He was all alone in the world. Until the day they introduced Perdrix, a she-wolf, into his cage.

To begin with, Blue Wolf wasn't too happy about this. He had grown used to being alone. He preferred his own memories for company.

The she-wolf wanted to ask a whole heap of questions. "What's your name?" She had grey fur and a muzzle that was nearly white. "Where do you come from?" Her paws were white too. "Did they capture you a long time ago?"

She's just like a snow partridge, thought Blue Wolf.

"Fine," said the she-wolf, "don't answer, if that's what you want. But I'm warning you: I'll answer you like a shot when you ask *me* a question!"

That's the kind of thing Shiny Straw would have said to me, thought Blue Wolf. So he enquired, "Where do *you* come from then?"

"From the Far North."

"It's a big place, the Far North..."

"I come from the barren lands, in Alaska."

Blue Wolf held his breath. The barren lands? That was the name humans gave to the place where he'd been captured. He could hear his heart pounding in his chest.

"The barren lands? Tell me, do you know—"

"I know everyone back there."

"Do you know a little she-wolf with golden fur?"

"Shiny Straw? The daughter of Black Flame and Great Wolf? Of course I know her! But, for one thing, she's not a little she-wolf any more – she's huge. Bigger than all the other wolves. And, secondly, she hasn't got golden fur now."

"Hasn't got golden fur? Now you're telling fibs."

"It's not a fib; I never lie. Of course, she *used* to have golden fur. But not any more. It stopped shining."

"Stopped shining?"

"Exactly. One night she left with one of her brothers – no one knows where they went – and the next morning she came back alone. The shine had gone from her fur; she no longer glowed in the sunshine. She's just Yellow Straw now! They say she's in mourning."

"That's what they say?"

"They say all sorts of things about her. And I know her well enough to be certain that everything they say is true. They say that no wolf has ever been a better hunter, and it's true. They say that neither she nor her family will ever allow themselves to be captured by humans, and it's true."

"How do you know?" asked Blue Wolf, who felt a huge ball of pride swelling in his chest.

So Perdrix told him. It happened one summer, when there were three families of wolves gathered round a pond that was swarming with ducks. Shiny Straw's family and Perdrix's family were there. Everyone was lying silently in wait, when suddenly they heard something whizzing above them, whoosh ... whoosh ... whoosh! It was a helicopter. ("Yes, they've started hunting us down with helicopters now.") Bang! Bang! The first shots rang out. Total panic! Wolves were trying to escape in every direction, as if the air current from the propeller blades was dispersing them. Fortunately the hunters weren't good marksmen. They were amateurs who just hunted for fun.

The helicopter was losing height. The grass below flattened out. But Shiny Straw was in the grass, although it was impossible to spot her because she was exactly the same colour. Then, out of the blue, she snapped at the pilot's leg. Ouch! The helicopter rose up again, spun round in a peculiar way and … splash! It landed in the middle of the pond.

"I rushed towards Shiny Straw. 'How did you manage that, Shiny Straw? Tell us how you did it.' And do you know what she said?"

"'My eyes!'"

"How do *you* know?"

"I'll tell you later. Finish the story first."

"Yes, the rest of the story… Well, there was the helicopter in the middle of the pond, and the men were splashing all the ducks – the ducks were hopping mad! – and the wolves were sitting on the bank, laughing so hard they were splitting their sides. You can't imagine how much they were enjoying themselves. Shiny Straw was the only one who wasn't laughing."

"She wasn't laughing?"

"No … she never laughs."

VIII

After their conversation Blue Wolf decided Perdrix wasn't such bad company after all. She was always in a good mood. They swapped memories; the years went by. And then, last week, Perdrix died. Which brings us up to date. Right up to the present moment, with Blue Wolf sitting in his empty enclosure, opposite the boy.

The pair of them stare into each other's eye. Their silence is framed by the distant rumbling from the town. How long have the boy and the wolf been staring at each other like this? The boy has watched the sun setting in the wolf's eye several times. Not the cold sun of Alaska (which gives off such a pale light you never know whether it's setting or rising), but the sun from here, the sun at the zoo, which disappears each evening when the visitors leave. Night falls in the wolf's eye. First of all the colours blur, and then the shapes get rubbed out. And the wolf's eyelid finally slides shut over his eye. The wolf stays sitting upright opposite the boy.

But he's fallen asleep.

The boy tiptoes out of the zoo, the way you might sneak out of a bedroom.

But each morning, when Black Flame, Grey Cousin, the Redheads, Shiny Straw and Perdrix wake up in the eye of the wolf, the boy is there again, standing in front of the enclosure, concentrating without moving a muscle.

Soon you'll know everything there is to know about me.

Now the wolf is gathering together even his tiniest memories: all the different zoos, all the sad animals he's met along the way who were prisoners like him, all the human faces he pretended not to see (faces that didn't look very happy either). He remembers the seasons passing by like clouds, the last leaf to fall from the tree, the final glance Perdrix gave him, the day he decided he wouldn't eat his meat any more.

Right up until Blue Wolf's last memory.

It was the moment when the boy arrived in front of his enclosure, one morning at the beginning of winter.

Yes, *you* are my last memory.

It's true. The boy can see his own image appearing in the wolf's eye.

You really annoyed me to begin with!

The boy can see himself, standing still as a frozen tree, inside that round eye.

I used to ask myself, What does he want from me? What's his problem? Hasn't he ever seen a wolf before?

The boy can see his breath creating a white mist in the wolf's eye.

I used to say to myself, He'll give up before I do; I'm more patient than he is – I'm the wolf!

But the boy in the wolf's eye doesn't seem to have any intention of leaving.

You know what? I was furious. To prove his point the wolf's pupil contracts and expands like a flame around the boy's image. And then you closed your eye. Which was a very kind thing to do...

Everything is calm now. The snow begins to fall gently over the wolf and the boy. The last snowflakes of winter.

But you? *You?* What kind of person a

Who are you? What are you called, for a start?

The Human Eye

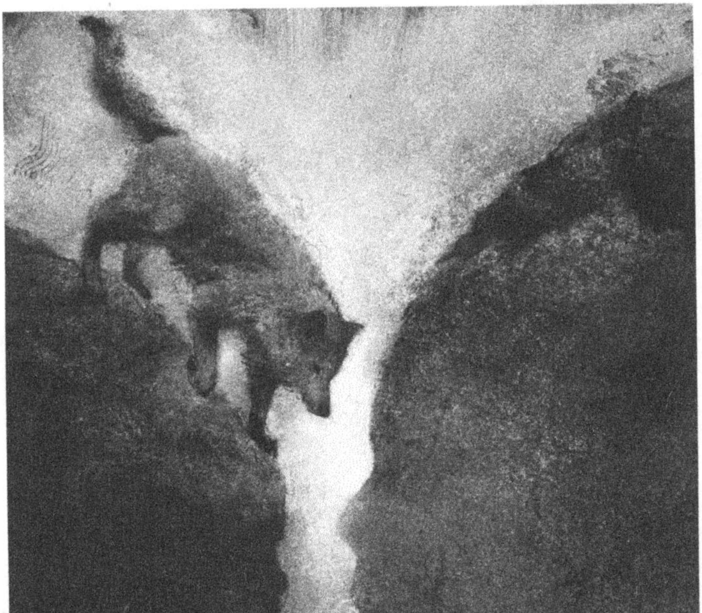

I

It isn't the first time he's been asked about his name. The other children had quizzed him to begin with.

"Are you new around here?"

"Where d'you come from?"

"What does your dad do?"

"How old are you?"

"What class are you in?"

"Do you know how to play bulldog?"

The sort of questions kids ask everywhere. But the most common question of all was the one the wolf had just asked silently, inside his head. "What are you called?"

And nobody ever understood the boy's answer.

"My name is Africa."

"Africa? That's not a person's name; it's the name of a country!" And they would laugh.

"But that's what my name is. Africa."

"Seriously?"

"You're joking!"

"You're pulling our leg, aren't you?"

The boy would look at them in a peculiar way and ask calmly, "Do I look like I'm pulling your leg?"

And the thing was, he didn't.

"Sorry, we were just having a bit of fun..."

"We wouldn't want to..."

"We didn't mean to..."

The boy would raise his hand and smile gently to show that no offence was taken.

"Right, Africa is my first name. And my surname is N'Bia. So I'm called Africa N'Bia."

But the boy knows that a name doesn't mean anything without the story that goes with it. It's like a wolf in a zoo: he's just another animal until you get to know his life story.

All right, Blue Wolf, I'll tell you my story.

And the boy's eye begins to transform itself in turn. It looks like a light being switched off. Or a tunnel going down into the earth. Blue Wolf squeezes into the tunnel, as if he's entering a fox's den. The further down he goes, the less he can see. Soon there isn't a glimmer of light left. Blue Wolf can't even see his own paws.

It would be difficult to say how long he burrows down into the boy's eye. The minutes go by like years. And then a whisper rises up out of the darkness.

Here we are, Blue Wolf; this is where my first memory took place!

II

It's a terrifying night. A moonless African night. You'd think the sun had never shone on Earth. And there's such a din. Panicked cries, flashes of light splitting the darkness in every direction, followed by a series of explosions: just like the night when Blue Wolf was captured. Then comes the crackling of flames. Black shadows are cast against the walls in the red glow. This is war, or something close to it. Everywhere you look, fires are blazing and houses are crashing down...

"Toa! Toa!" a woman calls out as she runs. She's carrying something in her arms and shouting out to a man who's sidling along the walls. He's leading an enormous camel by the reins.

"Toa the trader, please listen to me!"

"This is hardly the moment for idle chat."

"I haven't come to chat. It's for the child's sake, Toa. Take this child and lead him far away from here. He doesn't have a mother any more." She holds out the bundle in her arms.

"What do you want me to do with such a tiny child? He'll just drink all my water."

The flames suddenly leap out of a neighbouring window. Toa can smell his moustache getting singed. "Oh, Africa! Curse Africa!"

"I'm begging you, Toa, save the child. When he's older he'll become a storyteller; he'll tell stories to make people dream."

"I've no use for dreams; I've got enough problems on my hands with this idiot of a camel who does nothing but dream from morning to night."

The camel, who has been making his way through the scene of destruction as calmly as if it was an oasis, comes to a complete standstill.

"Toa!" shouts the woman. "I'll pay you."

"I'm not interested. Are you going to get a move on?"

"Lots of money, Toa, lots!"

"Stupid camel, every time I tell him he's an idiot, he refuses to budge. How much money?"

"Everything I've got."

"Everything?"

"Absolutely everything!"

III

Day breaks over a completely different landscape. Blue Wolf can't believe his eyes. Snow! There's not a tree or a rock or a single blade of grass in sight. Just snow. And blue sky. Big hills of snow, as far as the eye can see. A strange, yellow kind of snow that creaks and crunches with every step, and slides in patches like the snow in Alaska. In the middle of the sky there's a white sun so bright it blinds people, and it makes Toa the trader drip with sweat.

"Curse this desert! Curse this sand! Will it never end?" Toa is bent double as he walks. He leads the camel by the reins, and swears between his teeth. "Oh, Africa! Curse Africa!"

The camel doesn't listen to him. He moves on dreamily. Actually, he's not a camel – he's a dromedary. He's only got one hump. It's mind-boggling what Toa has managed to pile onto his back! Saucepans, boilers, coffee grinders, shoes, paraffin lamps, rush-stools: he's like a walking ironmonger's shop, rattling with every bump of his hump. And up there, right on top of the heap, sitting bolt upright and wrapped in a Bedouin coat, is the boy. He gazes into the distance.

There you are, thinks the wolf. I was worried that crook would desert you.

Blue Wolf has every reason to be concerned. Many years have slipped by since that dreadful night, and Toa the trader has tried to abandon the boy many times. He always goes about it in the same way. On certain mornings, when he's in a particularly foul mood (business is bad; the watering place has run dry; it's been a cold night ... there's always an excuse), he gets up without making a noise, rolls up his brown wool tent and whispers in the ear of his dozing camel, "Let's get going, camel. Up you get. We're off."

The boy pretends to be asleep. He knows what'll happen next.

"Are you coming then?" Toa the trader pulls on the bridle while the dromedary looks at him and chews an old thistle. "Are you going to get up, or what?"

No. The dromedary stays slumped on his knees. At this point Toa always brandishes a big knobbly stick. "Is this what you want?" But when the dromedary rolls back his chops and bares his big flat yellow teeth, the stick always falls to the ground.

I'm not leaving without the boy. That's what the dromedary is saying behind his silence and his stillness and his calm gaze.

So Toa goes over to wake up the boy with a sharp slap. "Come on, get up! I'm late enough as it is because of you. Climb up there and don't move an inch."

The dromedary won't allow anyone else on his back. So the boy always rides up above and Toa the trader stays down below, walking on foot through the burning sand.

"Good morning, Sand Flea, did you sleep well?"

"Sound as Africa! And you, Saucepans, did you have a good night?" (The boy's nickname for the dromedary is Saucepans.)

"Slept like a log, and I had very interesting dreams."

"Right, are we off?"

"Let's go."

Saucepans unfolds his legs and stands up against the orange sky.

The sun rises. Toa the trader swears and spits and curses Africa. The dromedary and the boy chuckle. They learned how to laugh on the inside a long time ago. Seen from the outside, they are both as smooth and serious as sand dunes.

IV

So that was the first chapter of his life. Even if he'd scoured all of Africa, Toa the trader would never have found a boy faster at loading and unloading the dromedary. He'd never have found someone better at arranging the merchandise in front of the Bedouin tents, someone who understood the camels more deeply, or, most importantly, someone who could tell such incredible stories at night, around the fires, when the Sahara becomes as cold as a desert of ice and you feel all alone in the world.

"He tells them well, doesn't he?"

"He's a good storyteller, isn't he?"

"It's the way he tells them!"

His stories attracted customers from the nomad camps. Toa was happy.

"Eh! Toa, what do you call your boy?"

"Haven't had time to give him a name – too busy working."

The nomads didn't like Toa the trader. "Toa, you don't deserve this boy." They would offer the boy a seat near the brazier, feed him with boiling tea, dates and milk curds (they thought he was too thin), and they would say, "Tell us a story."

So the boy would tell them stories he had made up in his head while he was sitting on Saucepans' hump. Or else he would tell them the dromedary's dreams, because the dromedary dreamed every night and sometimes he even dreamed while he was walking in the sunshine. They were stories about Yellow Africa, about the Sahara, about an Africa filled with sands and sunshine and solitude and scorpions and silence. And when the caravans set out again under the blazing sky, those who had listened to the boy's stories saw a different Africa from high up on their camels. In this new Africa the sand was gentle underfoot, the sun was a fountain, and they were no longer alone: the young boy's voice followed them wherever they went in the desert.

"Africa!"

It was during one of these nights that an old Tuareg chief, who was at least a hundred and fifty years old, declared, "Toa, we'll call this boy Africa!"

Toa stayed back and sat on his coat while Africa was telling his stories. But he would get up at the end of each story and hold out a tin bowl to collect bronze coins or old notes.

"He's even got the nerve to charge us for the boy's stories."

"Toa the trader, you'd sell *yourself* if someone was willing to pay for you."

"I'm a trader," Toa would grumble. "It's my job to sell things."

They were right when they said that Toa would sell everything he had. And one fine morning he did just that.

It happened in a town in the south where the desert sands run out. It's a different Africa. Grey. With burning stones and thorny bushes and, further south still, great plains of dried plants.

"Wait here for me," Toa had ordered. "Guard the tent."

And he had disappeared off into the town, leading his camel by the reins. Africa was no longer frightened of being abandoned. He knew that

Saucepans would never leave town without him.

But when Toa returned, he was alone. "I've sold the camel."

"What do you mean? You've sold Saucepans? Who to?"

"None of your business." There was a strange glint in his eye. "Oh, and by the way, I've sold you too." And he added, "You're a shepherd now."

V

After Toa left, Africa spent hours searching for Saucepans. But it was no use.

He can't have left town; he wouldn't have taken a single step without me. He promised!

He questioned passers-by.

"Little one, there are two thousand camels sold here every day," they replied.

He asked children his own age. "You wouldn't have seen a dromedary who dreams, by any chance?"

The children laughed. "All dromedaries dream."

He even interrogated the camels themselves. "A dromedary who's as tall as a sand dune!"

The camels looked down on him from a great height. "There are no dumpy dromedaries in our crowd, boy, only beautiful beasts..."

And of course, he also approached the camel buyers. "A handsome dromedary the colour of sand, sold by Toa the trader..."

"How much?" the buyers asked, because they were only interested in prices.

This carried on until the king of goats lost his temper. "Now, listen up, Africa! You're not here to hunt for a dromedary; your job is to protect my flocks."

Toa had sold Africa to the king of goats. The king of goats wasn't a cruel master, but he loved his flocks more than anything in the world. His curly white hair was like sheep's wool; he ate nothing but goat's cheese and drank nothing but ewe's milk; and when he bleated his words the long hairs of his goatee beard wobbled. He lived in a tent instead of a house, to remind him of the times when he tended the flocks himself, and he never got up off the vast curly black sheepskin that was his bed.

"Yes, I'm too old now. Otherwise I wouldn't need a shepherd."

If a ewe fell ill or a ram broke his leg or a goat disappeared, he sacked his shepherds on the spot.

"Do I make myself clear, Africa?"

The boy nodded.

"Right, sit down and listen." The king of goats

held out a large piece of cheese and a bowl of milk that was still warm, and he taught him how to be a shepherd.

Africa worked for the king of goats for two whole years. The inhabitants of Grey Africa couldn't get over it. "The old man doesn't normally keep a shepherd for more than two weeks. What's your secret?"

But Africa didn't have any secret. He was a good shepherd, and that was all there was to it. He had grasped a basic principle: flocks don't have enemies. If a lion or a cheetah eats a goat from time to time, it's because he's hungry. Africa had explained this to the king of goats.

"King, if you don't want the lions to attack your flocks, you'll have to give them something else to eat."

"Feed the lions?"

The king of goats twiddled his beard. "All right, Africa, perhaps it's not such a bad idea."

So, wherever Africa led the goats to pasture, he laid out large chunks of meat he'd brought with him from the town. "Here's your share, Lion, so please leave my goats alone."

The old lion of Grey Africa took his time sniffing the chunks of meat. "You're a funny one, Shepherd, you really are a funny one." And then he tucked in.

Africa held a longer conversation with the cheetah. One evening when the cheetah was creeping cautiously towards the flock, Africa said, "It's no good pretending to be a snake, Cheetah – I heard you."

The astonished cheetah poked his head above the dry grass. "How did you know I was here, Shepherd? No one ever hears me!"

"I come from Yellow Africa. There's so much silence back there it sharpens our ears. Listen – I can hear two fleas arguing on your shoulder."

With one snap of his teeth the cheetah devoured both fleas.

"Right," said Africa, "I need to talk to you."

The cheetah was impressed so he sat down and listened.

"You're a good hunter, Cheetah. You can run faster than all the other animals, and you can see further too. Those are the skills a shepherd needs."

There was silence. They heard an elephant trumpeting in the distance; then came the sound of shots ringing out.

"Foreign hunters..." murmured Africa.

"Yes, they're back," said the cheetah. "I saw them yesterday."

They were sad and silent for a while.

"Cheetah, what about teaming up with me as a shepherd?"

"What's in it for me?"

Africa stared at the cheetah for a long time. Two old tears had left black stains that went right down to the corners of his mouth.

"You need a friend, Cheetah, and so do I."

And very soon Africa and the cheetah were inseparable.

VI

When the grazing areas were too far apart, the youngest goats couldn't keep up with the flock. They tired easily. They would fall behind and the hyenas, who were never far off, would lick their chops and cackle. The cheetah was fed up because he had to keep going backwards and forwards to fend off the hyenas. The most vulnerable kids were also very rare and beautiful; they were a special breed that the king of goats called "my Abyssinian doves". He spent sleepless nights worrying something might happen to them.

"King, I've had an idea about how to protect your doves. We should leave the youngest ones behind," Africa explained.

The king of goats plucked three hairs out of his beard. "Leave them behind where they'll be unprotected! Are you out of your mind? What about the hyenas?"

"That's just the point. If I leave the kids in the biggest thorny shrubs, the hyenas won't touch them."

The king of goats closed his eyes and thought quickly. Let's see ... all goats graze on thorns, they've got mouths made to grind nails, they've got thorn-proof fur, and if there's one thing hyenas can't stand it's thorns. There's no doubt about it – it's a great idea.

Turning to Africa again, he stroked his beard and asked, "Tell me, Africa, why didn't I have this idea before you did?"

Africa looked into the old man's pale, worn-out eyes and replied gently, "Because I'm the shepherd now. And you're the king."

The hyena's head contemplating a thorny shrub was a sight to see.

"It's just not fair, Africa, to have a goat right under my nose, and an Abyssinian dove at that! What a temptation! It's downright cruel of you." She was drooling so much that flowers could have sprung up between her paws.

Africa patted her on the forehead. "When I

come back, I'll bring you the old lion's leftovers. Lions are just like rich people – they never finish their food."

The cheetah didn't like the smell of the hyena and he frowned. "Shepherd, you shouldn't talk to *that*."

"I talk to everyone."

"You're making a mistake. I don't trust *that* one little bit."

The flock started moving again. The cheetah cast a final scornful glance at the hyena before announcing to Africa, "Not that it matters anyway. While I'm alive, no one will ever eat one of your goats."

The days turned to months and the flock prospered. The king of goats slept peacefully at night. Everyone was happy, including the hyena, who made a feast of the lion's leftovers. She even claimed to hover around the thorny shrubs in order to protect the Abyssinian doves. The cheetah would shake his head and look at the sky.

"It's the honest truth!" the hyena insisted. "If anything happened to the doves, Shepherd, I'd be the first to let you know!"

The little shepherd boy's fame spread throughout Grey Africa. He was very popular. When Africa lit his fires in the evening, a host of black shadows soon slid up to him. These weren't the shadows of robbers or ravenous animals. It was a crowd of men and beasts that gathered to hear the stories of Africa, shepherd boy to the king of goats. He told them about another Africa, Yellow Africa. He told them about the dreams of a dromedary called Saucepans, who had mysteriously disappeared. And he spun them tales of Grey Africa too, which he knew better than they did, even though he wasn't born there.

"He tells them well, doesn't he?"

"He's a good storyteller, isn't he?"

"It's the way he tells them!"

And when dawn came and everyone headed off in different directions, they felt they were still somehow together.

One day the grey gorilla of the swamps interrupted a story. "Did you know there's another Africa, Shepherd? Green Africa, filled with trees as high and puffy as clouds. I've got a cousin who lives there; he's a strapping fellow with a pointy skull!"

Green Africa? No one was very convinced. But they didn't want to argue with the grey gorilla of the swamps...

Life is strange... Someone tells you about something you didn't even know existed, something unimaginable, something you can't bring yourself to believe in, and the words are hardly out of their mouth before you find out all about it for yourself.

Green Africa... It was a place the boy would soon be very familiar with.

VII

One night Africa was telling a story and the animals were all listening, when the cheetah suddenly whistled. "Sshh!"

They could hear the hyena laughing far off in the distance. But it wasn't her usual laugh; it was a furious cackling...

"Something's happened to the Abyssinian doves!" The cheetah leaped to his feet. "I'm off! Meet me over there, Shepherd, and bring the flock with you." Then, just before disappearing, "I told you never to trust *that*."

In the small hours of dawn, when Africa reached the first thorny shrub, his heart stopped beating. The shrub was empty! The hyena had disappeared. And so too had the cheetah. The signs of a fight were plain to see... But no one had any idea what had happened.

The king of goats nearly died of shock. "My

favourite Abyssinian dove! She was the most beautiful goat I ever had. The daintiest. The apple of my eye. The finest pedigree. Now do you see what comes of making friends with cheetahs? He'll have eaten her. Curse you, Shepherd, you and your silly ideas about thorny shrubs. Be off with you! Out of my sight, before I strangle you."

Should he stay in Grey Africa? Out of the question. He'd feel too sad. What about going back to Yellow Africa? Not without Saucepans. Then the boy remembered the grey gorilla of the swamps and what he'd said about Green Africa. "I've got a cousin who lives there."

"And how will you pay for your journey?" the driver had asked him.

"I'll clean your lorry," Africa had replied.

"It doesn't need cleaning; the engine's what matters."

"I'll cook your meals for you."

"I'm already sorted for food." (The driver had shown Africa a store of black biscuits and white cheese.)

"I'll tell you stories."

"That's better; I like stories. And they'll stop me falling asleep. Climb up. If I get bored, I'll throw you out of the window."

So that's how they left Grey Africa. With the driver driving too fast and Africa telling his stories. But his mind was somewhere else while he was telling them. What had happened to the little goat? What had happened to the cheetah and the hyena? Am I going to lose all my friends, one after another? Is there something about me that brings bad luck?

The sun rose and set. It was a sad journey. A long journey. A long hot flat journey.

The lorry was actually a kind of small bus with rattling metal parts. Other passengers got on. The driver made them pay. He was charging a high price for the ride. ("I've got a boy storyteller.") Lots of people got on. Far too many, as Africa pointed out to the driver.

"You're overloaded, and you're driving too fast!"

"Stop nagging and tell your stories!"

So Africa told his stories night and day. At night a sea of eyes listened to him...

One morning everyone let out a great cry.

Over there, beyond the sea of dry and cracked earth, were the green rolling hills of the tropical rainforest. Green Africa! The grey gorilla of the swamps hadn't been lying.

Everybody pressed against the windows and whooped with joy. The driver accelerated again. They sped into the forest. And, inevitably, on a bend flanked by giant ferns, the little bus came off the road and turned over. There was a great din of clanging metal and the sound of the engine still roaring. With its four twisted wheels spinning in the air, the upturned bus looked like an old beetle on its back.

It was the last thing Africa saw before he lost consciousness.

VIII

"*Ma Bia, Ma Bia,* he's waking up!"

"Of course he's waking up. I've been taking care of him, haven't I?"

"All the same, he got better so quickly, I'd never have believed..."

"Pa Bia, how long have I been healing people?"

"At least fifty years, since you were a little girl."

"And how many of them didn't get better, Pa Bia?"

"None. They were all healed. It's a miracle every time..."

"It isn't a miracle; it's just the healing hand of Ma Bia!"

"All the same, I really thought this one was going to die."

"Silly old thing! This one is stronger than all the others; he'll live to be a hundred!"

Africa had been listening to their whisperings

and hushed laughs for some time now in his half sleep. It was time to open his eyes.

"Ma Bia, he's opening his eyes!"

"Yes, I can see he's opening his eyes. Give him some coconut milk."

Africa drank the milk. It was a cool, velvety sweet liquid with a slightly bitter taste. He liked it.

"He seems to like it."

"Yes, Pa Bia, I can see he likes it. He's drunk the coconut dry."

Africa fell asleep again.

When he woke up for the second time, the house was empty. But he could hear a voice speaking to him. "Hello there!" It was a metallic, nasal voice that seemed to come from a strange pale blue bird with a red tail and a beak made to smash nuts. The bird was perched on an earthenware jar.

"Hello," said Africa, "who are you?"

"I'm a parrot, and you?"

"I was a shepherd. I've also been a trader, well, kind of..."

"Really?" asked the parrot. "You're just like Pa

Bia then. And you'll probably end up working the land too."

"Can I go outside?" asked Africa.

"If you can stand on your own two legs, what's stopping you?"

Africa got up gingerly. But he needn't have worried, because he was completely cured. It was as if all the life that had drained out of him in the accident had come flooding back in his sleep. So he let out a whoop of joy and ran out of the house. But his whooping turned into a terrified screech. The house was propped high up on stilts: he'd just jumped into thin air.

Africa closed his eyes and waited for the crash. But it never came. Instead, two huge and unimaginably strong arms caught him in mid-flight, and he felt himself being crushed against a chest as wide and hairy and well padded as the king of goats' bed. Then came a peal of laughter so powerful that all the birds of the forest flew away in fright.

"Pa Bia, you could at least laugh a little bit more quietly."

"Think of all the animals trying to take their siesta."

The whole forest was in uproar.

"Ma Bia, look at him: he's completely cured." Pa Bia held Africa up in his arms and showed him to a tiny old woman who was emerging from the thick of the forest.

"There's no need to make such a hullabaloo, Pa Bia. I can see perfectly well that he's cured."

Africa's eyes nearly popped out of his head. The old woman was followed by a gigantic black gorilla with a pointy skull. He was carrying a large stash of pink papayas, which are the most delicious fruit and a natural remedy too.

"How strange," said the gorilla, "that Pa Bia has never been able to get it into his skull that you heal *everybody*!"

"Oh, be quiet, you big beast!" replied Ma Bia. "He's only pretending to be surprised because he knows I like it."

"Ah! I see..." said the gorilla.

IX

Pa and Ma Bia's house rose up on its four legs in the middle of the greenest clearing in the whole forest.

"Why is it on stilts?" asked Africa.

"So the snakes can't pay us a visit, little one."

There was a wall of forest foliage all around. It was so high you'd think you were at the bottom of a leafy well.

Pa and Ma Bia looked after Africa and fed him up. They never asked him any questions, and they didn't expect him to do any work. In the daytime they looked after the clearing and the trees. At night they sat around talking. They had experienced a great deal in their lifetimes. They knew all the people and all the animals in Green Africa. They had children and cousins scattered everywhere, throughout the three Africas and in the Other World too.

"The Other World? What's that?"

Pa Bia, who had just opened his mouth to answer Africa, was interrupted by the tumbling of broken branches and crushed leaves. The noise didn't come from nearby, but the tree that had just fallen was so tall the whole forest must have heard it come crashing down.

There was a long silence, and then Pa Bia said, "The Other World? Perhaps we'll be in the Other World sooner than we think..."

"Oh, be quiet," said Ma Bia. "Don't go putting ideas into the little one's head."

Africa began helping Pa and Ma Bia with their work, even though they hadn't asked him to. He went with them to gather the fruits of the forest, and every Saturday all three of them made the trip to the market in the small nearby town. Pa Bia was a good salesman who sold his fruit by shouting very loud. People also came to seek Ma Bia's advice; she charged a pittance and cured nearly all of them. But Africa was soon the most popular.

The moment their shopping was done, everybody gathered around him.

"He tells them well, doesn't he?"

"He's a good storyteller, isn't he?"

"It's the way he tells them!"

"And what about your own story, the story of your life – why don't you tell us that?"

It was a rainy day when Pa Bia asked this question. The rain was coming down in torrents. It was the right kind of weather for telling your life story. Pa and Ma Bia listened to Africa and nodded seriously.

"So you don't have a father?" asked Pa Bia when Africa had finished.

"I don't have a father, no."

"And you don't have a mother either?" asked Ma Bia.

"No, I don't have a mother either."

There was an embarrassed silence, because the same idea had just occurred to all three of them at the same time.

So Africa N'Bia became the youngest child of Pa and Ma Bia, who already had fourteen children, scattered throughout the Africas and the countries of the Other World.

X

But as the years went by, more and more trees fell. The forest was thinning out. And Pa Bia's forehead was getting more and more wrinkled.

"Don't worry, they'll stop one of these days."

But Ma Bia knew they would never stop.

In the rainy season, felled trees were thrown into the rivers that flow out to sea. One day Africa and the gorilla were sitting on the river bank, watching the stripped trunks drift by, when the gorilla let out a big sigh. "Soon there won't be any left."

Africa decided it was time to change the subject and asked, "Did you know you've got a cousin in Grey Africa?"

"A small fat one with a flat skull, in the swamps? Yes, I know," replied the gorilla, his mind on other things.

They sat in silence. And the sound of axes rose

up out of the silence.

"Where are all these trees going, anyway?" asked Africa.

The gorilla carried on staring at the river. "Where do you *think* they're going? To the Other World, of course!" And he added, as if for his own benefit, "Gracious me, I need to make a decision. I've got to make up my mind, and that's all there is to it."

"Me too," came a peculiar voice from nearby. It was a deep, pale whisper that sounded muffled.

"Why should it bother you?" asked the gorilla. "You don't live in the trees."

"Exactly," replied the crocodile. "I live in the water, and the trees are clogging it up."

Pa Bia made a decision too. "Come on," he said, "we're going."

"Why?" asked Africa.

Pa Bia drove him to the forest's edge and pointed out the great stretch of dry cracked earth that Africa had crossed for endless days and nights in the truck.

"Not so long ago," said Pa Bia, "the forest stretched all the way to the horizon. Today, all the trees have been cut down. And when there are no more trees, it stops raining. Can't you see there's nothing growing? The earth is so hard a dog couldn't bury his bone in it."

Suddenly Pa Bia pointed straight in front of him. "Look!"

Africa followed his finger, and saw something small and black and gleaming. It looked furious as it made its way obstinately towards the forest, brandishing a curved knife above its head.

"Even the black scorpion can't cope with this dryness." Pa Bia fell silent. A gust of scorching air raised a cloud of dust.

"This is what will become of our clearing." His lips were dry. "Come on," he said. "Let's get going."

The Other World

I

And that's how Pa Bia, Ma Bia and their son Africa came to join us in the Other World. They had a cousin in our town. Their cousin spread out a newspaper and helped Pa Bia look for work. Pa Bia would have turned his hand to anything, but there were hardly any jobs advertised.

"Don't worry," said Ma Bia, "we'll find something."

And, sure enough, one day their cousin did find something. "There," he said, ringing a small newspaper ad with a pen. "That's what you're looking for!"

So Pa Bia found a job with the zoo's tropical hothouse department. "What's a tropical hothouse?" he'd asked.

"It's a kind of glass cage, where they keep our trees from Green Africa," his cousin had replied.

The trees were almost dead; Pa Bia brought them back to life.

• • •

Africa would never forget the day he visited the zoo for the first time. He had no idea what it would be like. "It's a sort of garden filled with animals," Ma Bia had said. Africa didn't understand how you could plant animals in a garden. And he felt very sad. He missed the clearing and Green Africa. The walls of our town seemed a prison to him. He was alone in the world. All alone...

But he'd hardly set foot inside the gates when a familiar voice stopped him in his tracks. "Hello, Sand Flea! So you found me in the end? I knew you would."

Africa was speechless for a few seconds. He could not believe his eyes or ears. It was too fantastic to be true. "Saucepans!"

Yes. The dromedary was there, standing in front of him, in the middle of an enclosure circled with iron bars.

"Saucepans! What are you doing here?"

"Can't you see? I've been waiting for you. I haven't taken a single step since Toa sold me."

"Not one step?"

"I kept my promise. All sorts of people tried to make me walk, but I wasn't having any of it. I haven't put one foot in front of another since we were separated."

Africa's heart had almost stopped beating and he still couldn't believe his eyes. "So how did you get here then?"

Saucepans laughed quietly, on the inside. "What use is a crippled camel to a buyer?"

Africa was indignant. "You could have been beaten alive!"

"Oh no, my buyer preferred to sell me."

"Who to?"

"Does it matter? To another buyer ... who sold me again in turn."

"And then what?"

"And so on, from buyer to buyer, until I ended up being bought by a zoo supplier. A dromedary who wouldn't budge was exactly what he was looking for. He paid an awful lot of money for me."

He chuckled on the inside again. "I've travelled far and wide to get here, by boat, by train, by truck and even by crane! They lowered me by crane into the middle of the enclosure. Not a single step without you, Sand Flea! I didn't take a single step."

I'm going to cry, Africa said to himself. I just can't help it. I'm going to cry.

"But now I'll be able to stretch my legs at long last," snorted Saucepans. And he suddenly started jumping up and down on the spot. Then he galloped the length of his cage at breakneck speed, before rolling in the dust and balancing on his hump. With his legs in the air, he twirled around like a spinning top and roared with laughter.

His laughter was so infectious that it spread from cage to cage and animal to animal, until it came back round to Africa. The animal with the loudest laugh shouted, "Hey! Dromedary! Who d'you think you are? An Abyssinian dove?"

That laugh, thought Africa. I recognize that laugh.

Ten metres away, behind thick iron bars, the hyena from Grey Africa was laughing louder than all the other animals. "What's up, misery guts? Why aren't you laughing?" she asked the animal in the next cage. "Look at the dromedary!"

"I haven't got time to enjoy myself," came a voice that Africa recognized instantly. "I'm a shepherd, and it's my job to keep an eye on that goat." And the sad voice added, "In any case, if you'd kept a better eye on her yourself we wouldn't be here in the first place."

"I did all I could," the hyena complained, "so stop pretending you're a better shepherd than me."

Africa ran to the scene of the argument, where he stopped dead in his tracks. He took a deep breath before whispering, "Hello, Cheetah, is it you she's calling misery guts? Don't be sad any more; I'm here now."

"Hello, Shepherd. I'm not sad, just a bit tired. I haven't taken my eye off the dove since the moment the hunters captured her and *that*."

Africa smiled at the hyena, who looked rather embarrassed. "I did what I could, Africa, I promise you, but they used fresh meat to make a trap, and you know how difficult I find it to resist..."

"I deliberately got myself caught," said the cheetah, "in order to stay with the dove. Look at her – isn't she beautiful?" The cheetah motioned towards an enclosure ten metres away where the Abyssinian dove was gambolling radiantly in Africa's honour. "I haven't taken my eyes off her for one second," he repeated. "Day and night! But you're here at last, and I'll be able to have a rest." And he fell asleep on the spot.

• • •

They were all there. Africa caught up with all of them again in the zoo of the Other World. He saw the grey gorilla of the swamps and his cousin of the forest. ("What was I supposed to do? They were taking away my trees, so I decided to let them take me too. But they're such idiots – they've put my trees in one cage and me in another.") He saw the old lion from Grey Africa, the crocodile of the creeks, the blue parrot with his red tail and the angry little black scorpion, who had fled the drought and was brandishing his dagger behind the brightly lit glass of his tank. He even saw Toa the trader. He was selling ice creams now, but he hadn't changed at all. He kept getting his fingers caught in the candyfloss, and he spent his time cursing.

"Oh, the Other World. Don't talk to me about the Other World!"

Yes, Africa knew them all, all the inmates of the zoo. All except one.

II

"All except me?"

It's springtime now. The wolf and the boy are still opposite each other.

"Yes, Blue Wolf. You looked so sad and lonely..."

What a strange boy, thinks the wolf. What a strange human being! I wonder what Black Flame would have made of him?

But it's what the wolf can see in the boy's eye that surprises him most.

It is evening, and Pa and Ma Bia are standing in their kitchen. Africa is sitting opposite them on a stool. A yellow light bulb hangs from the ceiling. Ma Bia is holding the boy's head in her hands and tilting it. The boy only has one eye; the other one has been closed for months now. Even when he wakes up first thing in the morning, Africa only opens one eye.

Ma Bia shakes her head sadly. "No," she whispers, "I don't think I can cure him, not this time..."

Pa Bia sniffs and scratches his unshaven chin. "Perhaps we could try the doctor?"

So they try. The doctor prescribes drops. They make Africa's eyelashes so sticky you'd think he did nothing but cry from morning to night. But his eye doesn't open again.

They go back to the doctor. He's an honest man. "I don't understand it at all," he says.

"Me neither," replies Ma Bia.

I know exactly what's going on, thinks Blue Wolf. He is sorry to see Ma Bia hunched over the boy in the kitchen, and Pa Bia unable to sleep at night any more.

The boy just carries on watching him with his single eye.

Blue Wolf nods several times before asking, "How did you guess?"

Silence. The hint of a smile spreads across the boy's lips.

"All the same ... all the same ... I'd promised myself I'd keep that eye shut!"

The truth is, behind his closed eyelid the wolf's

eye has healed up a long time ago. But the combination of the zoo, the sad animals and the visitors... Pah! the wolf thought. One eye is quite enough to see all of that.

"Yes, Blue Wolf, but I'm here now!"

He's right. The boy's here now. He's told the animals from Africa all about the Far North. He's told Blue Wolf about the three Africas. And they've all begun to dream, even when they're wide awake!

For the first time Blue Wolf looks over the boy's shoulder, and he sees – *he can clearly see* – Shiny Straw and the cheetah cavorting around in the middle of the zoo, in the golden dust of the Sahara.

Soon Perdrix joins them, and the Redheads too, and they all begin dancing around the spinning-top dromedary. Pa Bia opens the doors of the hothouse, and the beautiful trees of Green Africa spill out onto the pathways. Grey Cousin and the gorilla of the rainforest are sitting next to each other, keeping watch from the highest branch.

And Blue Wolf can see the visitors, who haven't noticed what's happening. And the director of the zoo, who carries on doing his rounds. And Toa the trader, who's running at full pelt because he's being chased by the angry scorpion. And the children, who wonder why the hyena is laughing so loudly. And Black Flame, who's just sat down next to the boy and opposite Blue Wolf. He can see snow falling in the middle of spring, the silent and beautiful Alaskan snow spreading a blanket over everything and keeping secrets hidden...

Now that, thinks Blue Wolf, is almost worth seeing with both eyes.

Click! goes the wolf's eye as it opens.

Click! goes the boy's eye.

"I don't understand it at all," the vet will say later.

"Nor do I," the doctor will probably add.

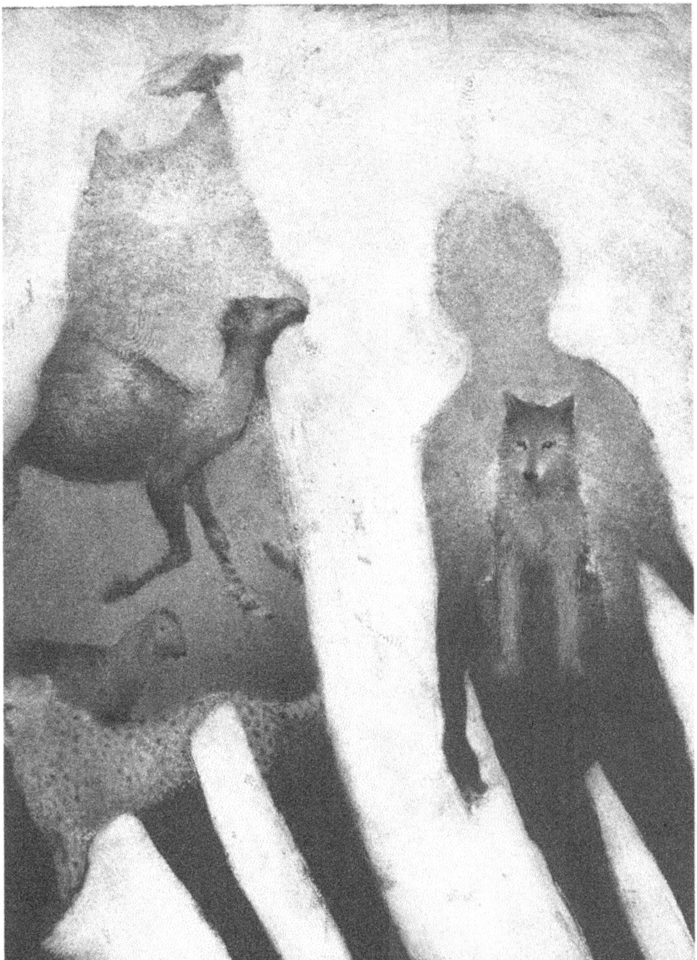

Daniel Pennac

The Rights of the Reader

The Rights of the Reader has sold over a million copies in France, and grew from Daniel Pennac's experiences of teaching in "challenging" schools. Central to the book is his belief that readers have rights: to read what, how, where and when they want, and – if they choose – the right NOT to read. Translated by the award-winning Sarah Ardizzone and introduced, and illustrated by Quentin Blake.

"A wonderfully economical and witty exploration of why we read and why we don't." *Guardian*

Daniel Pennac
Dog

Nearly drowned at birth, left for dead on a rubbish tip and hounded by dog-catchers – Dog's puppyhood is tough. All alone in the world, he decides to find himself an owner, someone he can train and love. Eventually he meets Plum, possibly the mistress of his dreams – but Dog must undergo many more adventures before he finds his happy ending in this funny, touching and wise tale.

"A book of distinction." *Guardian*

Timothée de Fombelle

Vango: Between Sky and Earth

Fleeing from the police and more sinister forces on his trail, Vango must race against time to prove his innocence. His journey will take him to the furthest reaches of distant lands, and even into the sky where he will find refuge on board the Graf Zeppelin airship. But the threat of war is getting closer, and Vango must uncover the secrets of his past before everything is lost.

"Exciting, unusual and beautifully written."

David Almond

Timothée de Fombelle

Vango Book Two: A Prince Without a Kingdom

Pursued by demons from his past, Vango scales the skyscrapers of New York on the trail of a man who holds the key to his identity. He has already sacrificed so much: abandoning those closest to him in a desperate bid to protect them from the evil that follows him. But Vango cannot run forever, and in the shadow of a rapidly changing world, the truth of his identity must finally come to light.

"An exceptional storyteller." *Libre Belgique*

WORLD VOICES

Timothée de Fombelle

Toby Alone

He's just one and a half millimetres tall, but Toby is the most wanted person in the great oak tree. Pursued across hazardous terrain of falling leaves, thick moss forests and bark mountains, hunted by an army of angry woodcutters and bloodthirsty soldier ants, Toby faces an epic battle for survival in an unforgettable miniature world.

"Imaginatively rich and great fun." *Guardian*

Timothée de Fombelle

Toby Alone and the Secrets of the Tree

The world of the great oak Tree is on the brink of devastation under the control of the power-crazed Leo Blue who is inflicting fear and poverty throughout the Tree and capturing anyone who tries to defy him. But Toby has returned – and he will find a way to fight back.

"An unprecedented success." *Le Figaro*

WORLD VOICES

Maria Parr

Waffle Hearts

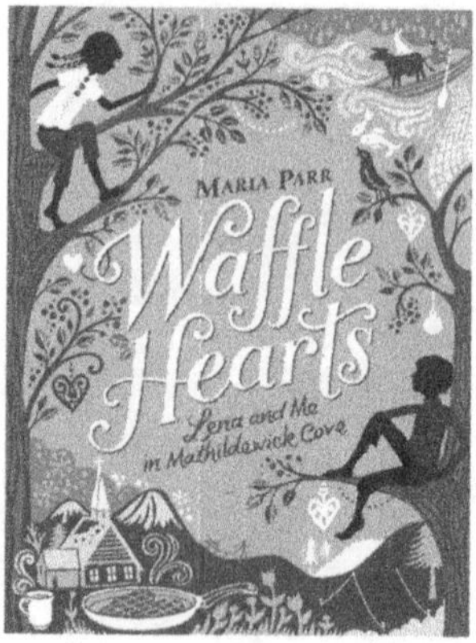

Whether it's putting a cow in a boat or advertising for a dad, no day is ordinary with a best friend like Lena.

Trille loves to share everything with her, even Auntie Granny's waffles. But when Lena faces a secret she can't share, will their friendship end?

Michael Morpurgo

Singing for Mrs Pettigrew

A wonderful and unique collection of stories and the story of their making; an engaging insight into the craft of one of today's most loved storytellers.

"From the first sentence of a Michael Morpurgo book, you know you are in the hands of a natural storyteller." *Guardian*

Daniel Pennac, novelist and thriller writer, is one of France's most celebrated authors. Widely regarded as a literary phenomenon, his books for both adults and children have been translated into over thirty languages and are read all over the world. His other books for Walker include *Dog* ("A book of distinction." – *Guardian*), *Kamo's Escape* and *The Rights of the Reader*, his sympathetic and witty guide to reading which has sold over a million copies in France. Daniel Pennac lives in Paris.

Sarah Ardizzone (née Adams) is one of the most sought after translators working today. She has won several awards for her work, including twice receiving the Marsh Award for children's literature in translation: in 2009 for *Toby and the Secrets of the Tree* by Timothée de Fombelle and in 2005 for *Eye of the Wolf* by Daniel Pennac. Sarah's latest projects include the award-winning Vango series by Timothée de Fombelle. Sarah promotes translation as a creative process in schools and beyond.

WORLD VOICES

"Our children need to be exposed to a world of voices so that the whole world becomes their home."

David Almond